Fire Down the Pit

Stories linking with the History National Curriculum Key Stage 2.

First published in 1998 by Franklin Watts
96 Leonard Street, London EC2A 4RH

Editor: Matthew Parselle
Series editor: Paula Borton
Designer: Kirstie Billingham
Consultant: Dr Anne Millard
With thanks to Robert Protheroe-Jones at the Welsh Industrial and Maritime Museum.

A CIP catalogue record for this book is available from the British Library.

ISBN 0 7496 3091 4

Dewey Classification 942.9

Printed in Great Britain

Fire Down the Pit

by

Andrew Matthews

Illustrations by Stephen Lewis

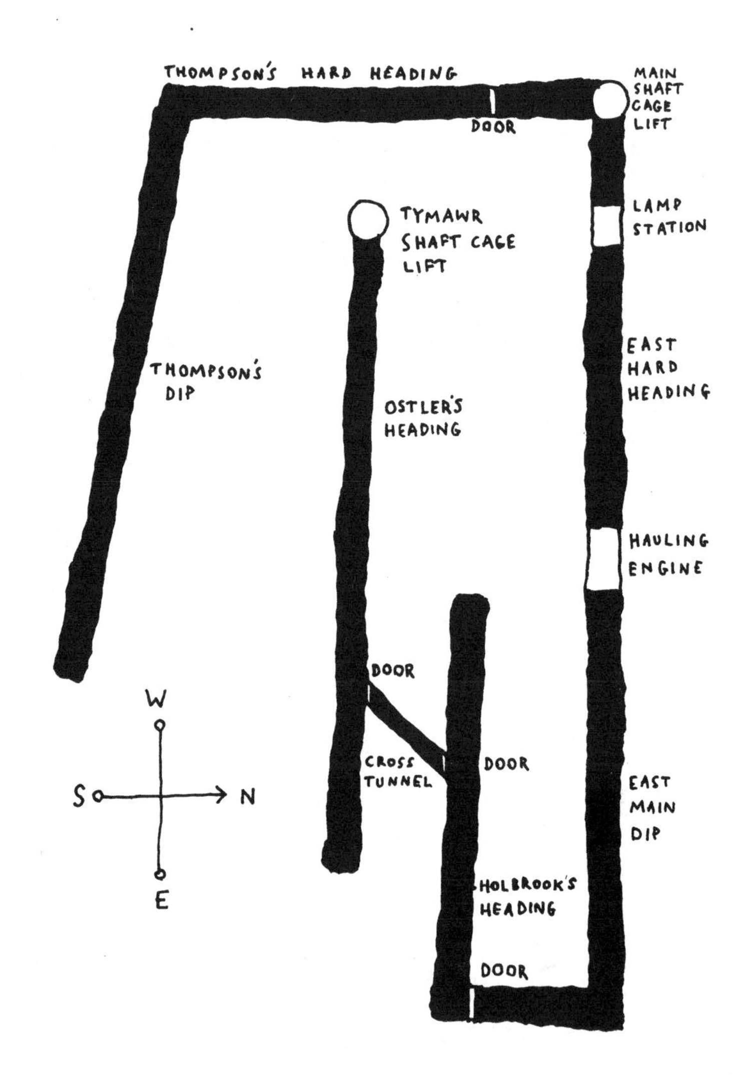

SIMPLIFIED MAP OF GREAT WESTERN COLLIERY APRIL 1893

1

Gwyn

Gwyn couldn't sleep. First it was the chuffing and clanking of the trains carrying coal through the night. Then his sister Megan had a bad dream and pulled the blankets over to her side of the bed. After that, one of the twins started crying, and that set the other one off. The twins were next door, in Mam and Dad's room, but the walls were so thin that Gwyn heard the bed-springs creak as Mam got up. She made cooing noises until the babies were quiet.

From across the town came the chiming of a clock. Gwyn counted the hours as the deep bell rang out. Ten o'clock. Two miles away and four hundred metres underground, Dad would be finishing his shift at the pit.

'That's where I'll be tomorrow!' Gwyn thought, and a cold, excited feeling made him sit up and hug his knees.

Tonight, he was still a boy, but tomorrow he would be a man, a worker at the Great Western Colliery.

Gwyn didn't feel like a man yet. He'd thought that once his birthday came, he would be a grown-up and things would be different. But he was the same Gwyn Parry who had been caned in front of the whole school for fighting in the playground. He still had a blue scar on his left knee from where he had fallen over when he was playing on a slag heap, and he could still remember the clip round the ear Old Ma Hewitt had given him when she caught him playing Knock-Down Ginger.

He didn't look grown-up either. After supper, Gwyn had gone into the scullery and peeped into the bit of broken mirror that Dad used when he was shaving.

It was the same face the mirror had always shown him – a squashed-up nose, like Mam's, and Dad's brown eyes and black curly hair. Gwyn had rubbed his face, hoping he had grown whiskers, but his skin was smooth – 'smooth as a babby's backside' as Dad would have said.

So when *would* he be grown-up? After his first day down the pit? Or would it be when he brought home his first pay-packet and put it on the parlour table, the way that Dad always did? The questions went round and round in Gwyn's head, like train-wheels...

The clock struck quarter-past eleven.

Gwyn slipped out of bed, pulled his trousers on over his night shirt and crept downstairs to wait for Dad.

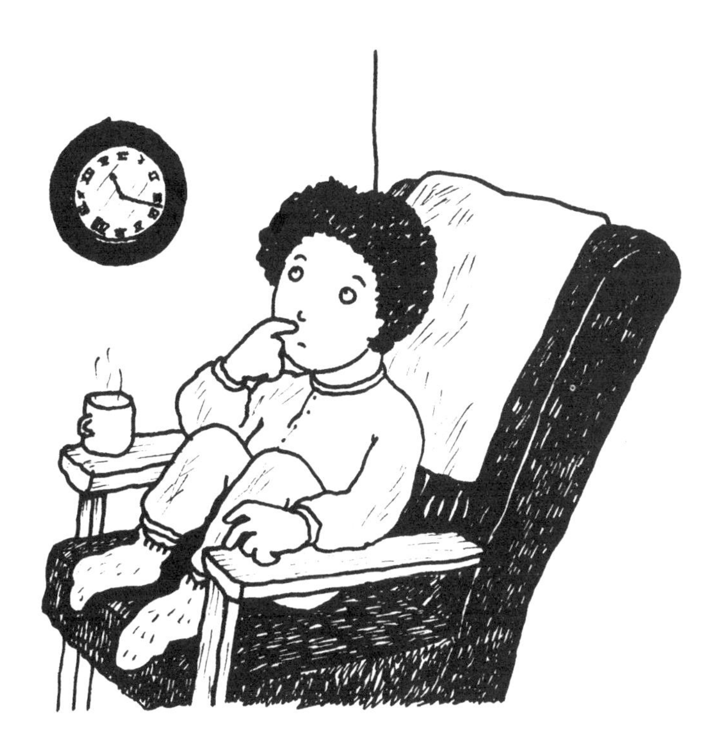

It was cosy in the parlour. Mam had left the gas light turned down low. Gwyn curled up in the chair next to the black-iron range and listened to the coal popping and tinkling as it burned in the fireplace. Dad's supper was keeping warm in a tin plate in the bottom oven. On the wall facing Gwyn, Grampy and Nanna Parry stared down from a photograph. Grampy looked like Dad, only with a bristly beard. Nanna looked sad. They had both died before Gwyn was born.

Grampy had been crushed by a roof-fall in a colliery just outside Rhymney, and Nanna had died of typhoid fever not long after. Gwyn wondered what they had been like, and he had almost imagined the sound of Grampy's voice, when the front door opened and Dad came in.

Dad's face was covered in coal dust that made him look like a sooty ghost.

He blinked at Gwyn, and his eyelids showed pink. 'What you doing up, boy?' he said.

'I can't sleep,' said Gwyn. 'I keep thinking.'

'You want to mind,' said Dad. 'Too much thinking wears your brains out!'

Dad went into the scullery to wash. When he came back, he smelled of soap and his face and hands were clean. Dad took his supper out of the range, and poured himself a mug of beer from the bottle on the dresser.

'Big day for you tomorrow, butty-bach!' he said.

'I know,' said Gwyn. 'That's what I keep thinking about.'

'You'll be all right,' said Dad. 'There's coal in your blood, like mine and your Grampy's. He started down the mines when he was ten years old, working on his hands and knees, pulling coal carts. Them was the bad old days!'

Gwyn watched his father eating for a while, then said, 'Dad, when d'you know you've grown up?'

Dad laughed and said, 'Duw! There's a question to ask me at this time of night!'

'But when do you?' said Gwyn.

Dad took a long drink of beer. 'I'll tell you, boy,' he said. 'When you're a kiddy, you can go skylarking from dawn to sundown without a care in the world. But when you're a grown-up, you get tired. It's work, eat, sleep and then back to work, day in and day out. That's what it seems like, anyway.'

Gwyn frowned. He had thought that growing up was something to look forward to – now he wasn't so sure.

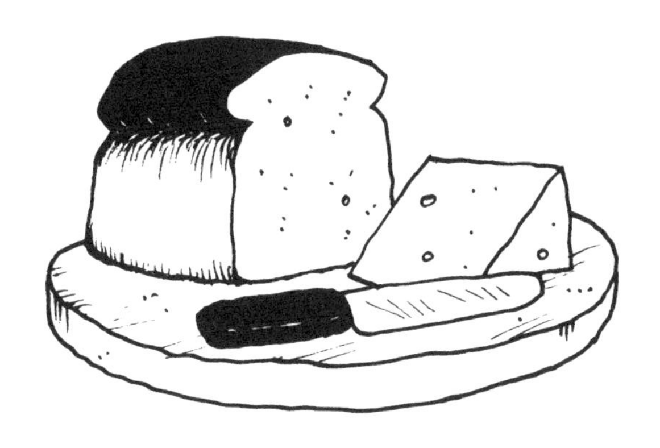

2

A Part of It

Gwyn got up late next morning, long after Megan had left for school. He put on a white flannel shirt, a pair of corduroy trousers, woollen socks and his new work boots.

Mam was in the parlour, her face red

from the heat of the range. She was stirring the porridge pot, frying slices of bread and holding on to Evan, one of the twins. The other twin, Morgan, was at her feet, staring at a black beetle as it scuttled across the floor.

'Where's Dad?' said Gwyn.

'On the privy. He'll be back now, directly,' Mam said. She spooned thick

grey porridge onto a plate and gave it to Gwyn.

'I can't eat all that!' he said.

'You get it down you,' said Mam. 'You'll do a man's work today, and you'll need a man's breakfast inside you.'

While Gwyn was blowing on his porridge to cool it, Dad came in through the back door. He picked up Morgan

and cooched him. 'See your big brother there?' Dad said. 'He's going to work down the pit today with your Dad.'

'Da!' gurgled Morgan.

'All right, boy?' Dad said to Gwyn.

'I've got the wind up a bit,' Gwyn said.

'It'll pass,' said Dad. 'My first time down a colliery, I was shaking like a leaf, mun.'

'What, *you?*' said Gwyn. He was surprised, because he didn't think that Dad had ever been frightened of anything.

'Plenty to be scared of down a pit, see,'

said Dad. 'Keep your wits about you, and trust the men you're working with. That's how you stay alive.'

Dad and Gwyn left for work at a quarter past twelve. They both wore black waistcoats and donkey jackets,

white scarves round their necks and flat caps on their heads. Gwyn carried his snap tin under his right arm. Inside the tin was a piece of bread and a hunk of cheese. In the left pocket of his jacket was a bottle of cold tea.

Dad breathed in deeply. 'Get some fresh air while you can,' he said. 'It'll be a long time before you smell it again.'

Gwyn filled his lungs and looked around. It had rained earlier, but now the sun was out, shining on the roofs of the houses that lined the sides of the valley.

Down in the valley, a train hauled along a long line of coal-trucks. Gwyn knew from school that the coal would be loaded onto ships at Barry Docks and Cardiff Docks, and then taken all over the world to power factories, battleships and ocean liners.

He was going to be a part of it. The coal that came out of the ground today might find its way to Canada, India or Australia – places he would never visit.

Gwyn could see the River Rhondda, and the colliery beside it.

The engine house snorted out billows of steam. Above the steam stood the black tower of the winding gear.

Gwyn thought it was strange that the town would still be there while he was working.

Mam would do a bit of cleaning and shopping, as usual, then Megan would come home from school, and all the time he would be deep underground.

'Like being asleep,' Gwyn told himself. 'When you're asleep the world goes on, but you don't know anything about it.'

His insides suddenly felt as though they had been filled with slithering eels.

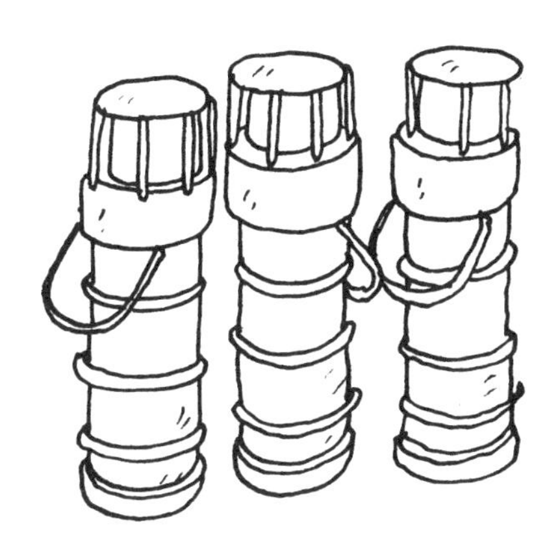

3

A Glow in the Dark

At the pit-head, Gwyn was given a safety lamp, and then he and Dad joined the queue of miners waiting for the cage lift.

'You'll have your lamp lit down below at the lamp station,' said Dad. 'Keep an eye on the flame inside the glass, and if

you ever see it
with a blue cap, run like fun!'

'Why?' said Gwyn.

'Fire damp,' said Dad. 'It's a gas that leaks out through the coal. You can't see it and you can't smell it, but if enough of it mixes with the air, it can cause an explosion.'

Gwyn followed Dad into the cage. When it was full, the door was pulled shut, the winding gear started and the cage lurched downwards. Earth and rock flashed past and then there was a darkness as thick as velvet.

Gwyn's heart beat faster. He seemed to feel the weight of the earth pressing down on him, grinding his bones and squeezing the air out of his lungs. A sharp pain in his ears made him gasp.

'Easy!' Dad said softly. 'That's the pressure. Just swallow hard.'

Gwyn swallowed. There was a crackling sound in his ears, and the pain vanished.

At the bottom of the shaft, Gwyn stepped out of the cage into a strong wind that made him shiver with cold. 'Where's the wind coming from, Dad?' he asked.

'There's a big fan up top that blows air down,' said Dad. 'It goes right through the mine, and goes up the shaft at Tymawr on the other side of the colliery. It gets warmer further on. The men work stripped to the waist, and sweat comes dripping off them.'

'Will I have to strip to the waist?' said Gwyn.

Dad laughed. 'No,' he said. 'Let's find Tommy Rosser, over by the lamp station. He'll tell you what's what. And mind you call him Mr Rosser, now.'

The stall of the lamp station was lit by electricity. Mr Rosser was outside, talking to a group of miners. He was short and thin, with a hooked nose.

'So this is your boy then, Dai?' he said after Dad introduced him to Gwyn. 'Think we'll make a collier out of him?'

'Like father, like son,' said Dad.

He put his hand on Gwyn's shoulder. 'I'm off up Thompson's Dip,' he said. 'You go with Mr Rosser. I'll see you at the pit-head when the shift finishes. Good luck, boy!'

As Dad walked away from the light into the dark, Mr Rosser said 'Well, Gwyn, you're my new trapper.'

'What's that?' said Gwyn, and Mr Rosser explained.

In the tunnels of the mine there were doors that had to be closed to make sure the air from the fan blew the right way. It was the trapper's job to open the doors when men or coal carts came through, and make sure they were shut tight afterwards.

'We all depend on each other down here, see,' said Mr Rosser. 'If you don't keep your doors shut, the colliers at the coal face will run out of air, understand?'

'Yes, Mr Rosser,' said Gwyn.

'Good. Now let's clog on.'

Mr Rosser led the way along a tunnel strung with electric lamps.

The tunnel was called 'the roadway' and there were narrow rails in it, along which ran carts loaded with coal. The roadway sloped steeply upwards for a hundred and fifty metres, until it came to the hauling engine that pulled the coal carts along on ropes. The ropes wound onto two big steel-plated drums, shaped like cotton reels.

There was a young man in the driver's cab of the engine, and Mr Rosser stopped to talk to him. 'Hello, George,' he said. 'Will Palmer still off sick, then?'

'I'll be glad when he gets back,' said the young man. 'The noise of this engine is enough to send you deaf, mun!'

Just then, one of the drums began to shriek as it sprayed out a shower of orange sparks.

'Ease up on the brake, George!'

shouted Mr Rosser.

George reached down to pull a lever, and the sparks stopped. 'Thanks, Tommy,' he said. 'I can't see properly from this cab.'

'Then make sure you come out and check,' Mr Rosser said. 'That Number One Drum gets overheated.

That's why Will Palmer always keeps a bucket of water in the cab.'

Gwyn and Mr Rosser walked on, down into the East Main Dip towards the part of the mine known as Holbrook's Heading. Neither of them noticed the red glow under the drums of the hauling engine.

A cotton rag had fallen down onto the thick, oil-soaked beams that the engine rested on. The sparks from the brake of Number One Drum had landed on the rag, and it had begun to smoulder.

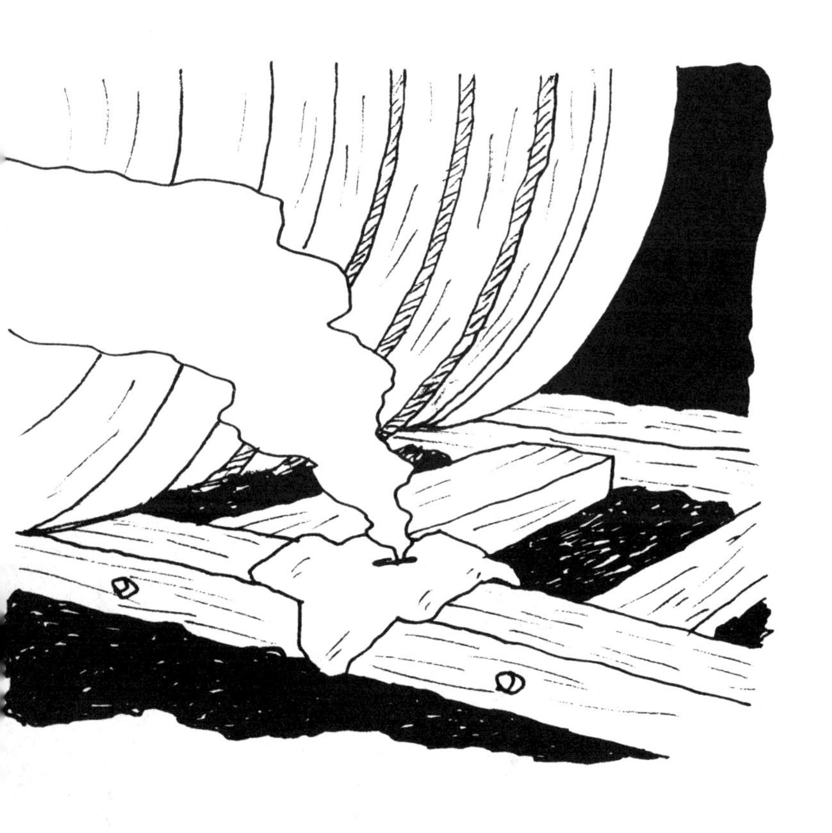

4

Fire!

Edwin Matthews was late for his shift at the Great Western pit, and didn't reach the bottom of the shaft until half-past two. He hurried from the lamp station up the roadway in the direction of East Main Dip. At the top of the slope, he came to a

halt and stood staring at the hauling engine. There was a strange light moving under the winding drums. Edwin sniffed, smelled burning oil and ran towards the engine, shouting, 'Fire!'

George came out of his cab, saw flames licking around the drums and ducked back inside for the bucket of water that stood near the doorway. He threw the water onto the blaze. The flames shrank back for a moment, then flared up again.

'We need more water!' cried Edwin. 'There's a stand-pipe back down the roadway. Quick!'

The two men raced down the slope of the tunnel to the stand-pipe, fifty metres away from the hauling engine.

Edwin turned on the tap while George held the bucket under the spout. The tap shook, spat out a thin trickle of water, then spluttered dry.

'What are we going to do?' groaned George.

'You fetch the under-manager,' said Edwin. 'I'm going to get the men out of Holbrook's Heading.'

'No you're not!' said George. 'Look!'

He pointed back towards the hauling engine. It was a mass of roaring flames that almost filled the tunnel, and the fire had spread to the wooden props that supported the roof. Clouds of thick black smoke were streaming down into the East Main Dip.

❖

At three o'clock a miner was sent up to the pit-head to fetch the mine manager. The miner was agitated, and unsure of what was going on, but what he had to say sent people scurrying in all directions.

Someone ran to the fan house and shouted, 'Accident below!'

'What kind of accident?' asked the fan-driver.

'There's fire and... an explosion! There must have been an explosion!'

The fan-driver thought quickly. He had been told about explosions underground, and he knew that there could be another one unless the mine was cleared of gas. 'Increase the speed of the fan to seventy-six revs!' he called to his crew.

Though the fan-driver meant well, it was the wrong thing to do. As the fan picked up speed, the wind in the mine blew at almost gale-force, and the fire in the hauling engine fed hungrily on the air.

Only closed lanterns were allowed near the coal face, so it was dark in Holbrook's Heading. The roof was too low for Gwyn to stand. He squatted in the pale circle of light from his safety lamp. He had only been working for an hour, but already his arms, legs and back ached.

He kept his eyes fixed on the doors, because if he looked beyond the light, his imagination played tricks on him and made him see things that weren't there, moving in the dark.

And there was a peculiar smell – like burnt bacon – that seemed to be growing stronger...

All at once, Gwyn heard a sound like wind sighing in the branches of a tree. The doors rattled on their hinges, as though someone were pushing against them.

Gwyn picked up his lamp, brought it close to the doors and saw smoke seeping underneath them. 'That can't be right, can it?' he thought. He wondered if he should go and find Mr Rosser, but he was afraid of making a fool of himself and besides, he had been told not to leave the doors – the colliers were depending on him. He glanced down, and saw that the smoke had risen to his knees.

'Something's wrong!' Gwyn said aloud. He turned and began to make his way up the tunnel, walking in a crouch, feeling his way along the wall with his right hand. Smoke reached his lungs, and he coughed.

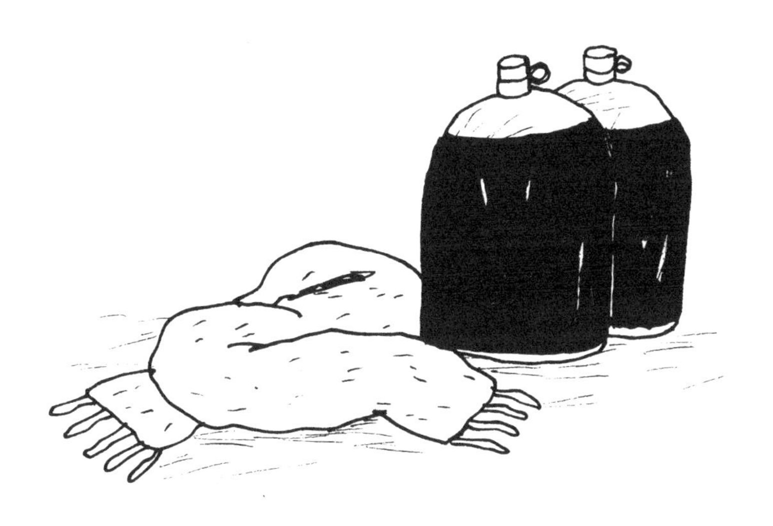

5

The Door

By ten past three, the mine was filled with smoke. Men staggered blindly towards the cages, their eyes streaming with tears. Some went in pairs, holding each other up, hacking and choking as they fought to breathe. Others collapsed as smoke overcame them, and lay unconscious on the ground.

At the pit-head, a pillar of black smoke rose into the air from the Tymawr shaft. Steam-whistles wailed out the alarm.

The mine manager burst into the fan house. 'Fire below!' he told the fan-driver. 'Shut off the fan! Hurry – there are more than seven hundred men down there!'

In Holbrook's Heading, the air was thick with smoke. The men gathered together, pooling the light from their closed lanterns.

'We've got to get out!' someone said.

'I'm off back up East Main Dip!' said another voice.

'No!' snapped Mr Rosser. 'Keep calm, boys! Wet your scarves with your drink-bottles, and tie them round your faces to keep the smoke out.

Davie Richards and I will go up the roadway and try to find out what's happening. Stay here till we get back!'

Gwyn found it hard work to breathe through wet cloth, but it helped a little.

Someone said, 'We're going to die!'

'Shut your row!' someone answered him. 'If anyone can get us out of this, it's Tommy Rosser.'

After that there was silence, except for the sound of some of the men muttering prayers.

Mr Rosser and Davie returned, coughing and spluttering.

'There's a fire between us and the main shaft,' Mr Rosser said.

'Then we've had it!' said the man standing next to Gwyn.

'We've still got a chance,' said Mr Rosser. 'Further up the workings, there's a cross-tunnel into Ostler's Heading.

We can get to the Tymawr shaft from there, if the smoke's not too bad.'

The men set off in single file. Gwyn wondered about Dad – had he escaped from the mine, or was he trapped? Panic gripped Gwyn like a cold hand, then he seemed to hear Dad's voice saying, 'Steady, boy!' and it made him think of home. He imagined Mam, Dad, Megan and the twins around the parlour table, waiting for him.

'I won't be long,' Gwyn told them in his mind, and his fear turned into a longing to be above ground, breathing clean air.

The miners reached the door into the cross-tunnel, but when they pushed against it, it would only open part-way.

'There must have been a roof-fall,' said Mr Rosser.

'We'll never get through there!' groaned one of the miners. 'I'll go back for some picks to break down the door.'

'There's no time for that,' said Mr Rosser. 'Gwyn, can you squeeze through and unblock the door?'

Gwyn looked. The gap was narrow, but he realised that it was the men's only hope. 'I can try,' he said.

It was hard. The edge of the door scraped against Gwyn's chest. He was half-way into the tunnel when he felt himself stick fast. 'I'm going home!' Gwyn whispered. 'We're all going home!' He wiggled his shoulders, pushed with his legs and slipped through.

The darkness in the tunnel was total. It pressed in on Gwyn, and for a moment he thought of the thousands of tons of stone above his head. 'Mustn't panic!' Gwyn told himself. 'Do something to take your mind off it!' He knelt down and began to search the floor with his hands. His fingers touched a large rock at the foot of the door. Gwyn grasped it, heaved with all his strength and it rolled away.
'It's clear!' he shouted.

The smoke was thinner in Ostler's Heading, and it continued to thin on the long, dark way to the Tymawr shaft. In places, the roof was so low that the men had to walk crouched; in other places they stumbled over the bodies of the dead.

But at last, there was a glimmer of light.

It was dusk when Gwyn finally emerged from the mine. He found Mam and Dad waiting for him among the crowd at the colliery gates. Mam burst into tears and hugged Gwyn tightly.

'Oh, leave go, Mam!' said Gwyn. 'You're hurting the bruises on my back!'

On the way home, Dad told the story of how he had escaped from the smoke, and stayed at the cages, helping other men to safety. 'But sixty-three miners are still missing,' he said. 'There's not much hope they'll be found alive now.'

'I would have been one of them if it hadn't been for Mr Rosser,' said Gwyn. 'He was a real hero!'

Dad shook his head. 'Everybody who works down a pit is a hero,' he said. 'And don't you forget it!'

'I won't,' said Gwyn. 'Not ever.'

Notes

The Great Western Colliery

The incidents in this story are based on a disaster that happened at the Great Western Colliery near Pontypridd in the Rhondda Valley on Tuesday, April 11th 1893. The official inquiry into the accident mentioned the cool-headed bravery of Thomas Rosser, who saved the lives of all the men in Holbrook's Heading. 63 men died of suffocation.

The colliery was closed in 1980, but a pit a little further up the Rhondda Valley was preserved as the Rhondda Heritage Museum.

Children in the Mines

Until the Mines Act of 1842, children as young as eight, boys and girls, worked underground in mines for up to 14 hours a day, from six in the morning until eight at night. After 1842, girls were not employed in mines, and boys could not go underground until they were 14, though many lied about their age and worked as 'trappers' – or door-boys, as they were officially called – when they were 11 or 12.

Fire-damp

Fire-damp is a gas called methane. It is highly flammable, and when mixed with air and coal dust becomes explosive. The danger of an explosion in a mine could be reduced by water-sprinklers, which damped down the coal dust, but regulations limiting the amount of dust in mines did not come into force until 1920.

The worst mining disaster in South Wales happened at the Senghenydd Colliery in October 1913. 439 miners were killed in an explosion, caused by fire-damp.

Welsh Words

'Tymawr' is Welsh for 'Great House'.
'Duw' is Welsh for 'God' and is pronounced like the English word 'dew'.
'Cooch' means 'to cuddle'.

Sparks History

INVADERS AND SETTLERS

Viking Raiders
A Tale of a Norse Attack
0 7496 3089 2 (hbk)

TALES OF THE ROWDY ROMANS

1. The Great Necklace Hunt
0 7496 2221 0 (hbk) 0 7496 2628 3 (pbk)

2. The Lost Legionary
0 7496 2222 9 (hbk) 0 7496 2629 1 (pbk)

3. The Guard Dog Geese
0 7496 2331 4 (hbk) 0 7496 2630 5 (pbk)

4. A Runaway Donkey
0 7496 2332 2 (hbk) 0 7496 2631 3 (pbk)

TUDORS AND STUARTS

Captain Drake's Orders
A Tale of the Armada
0 7496 2556 2 (hbk) 0 7496 3121 X (pbk)

London's Burning
A Tale of the Great Fire of London
0 7496 2557 0 (hbk) 0 7496 3122 8 (pbk)

Mystery at the Globe
A Tale of Shakespeare's Theatre
0 7496 3096 5 (hbk)

TALES OF A TUDOR TEARAWAY

1. A Pig called Henry
0 7496 2204 4 (hbk) 0 7496 2625 9 (pbk)

2. A Horse called Deathblow
0 7496 2205 9 (hbk) 0 7496 2624 0 (pbk)

3. Dancing for Captain Drake
0 7496 2234 2 (hbk) 0 7496 2626 7 (pbk)

4. Birthdays are a Serious Business
0 7496 2235 0 (hbk) 0 7496 2627 5 (pbk)

SCOTTISH HISTORY

A Queen's Promise
A Tale of Mary Queen of Scots
0 7496 2589 9 (hbk) 0 7496 3125 2 (pbk)

Stranger in the Glen
A Tale about Rob Roy
0 7496 2586 4 (hbk) 0 7496 3123 6 (pbk)

A Dream of Danger
The Massacre of Glencoe
0 7496 2587 2 (hbk) 0 7496 3124 4 (pbk)

Over the Sea to Skye
A Tale of Bonnie Prince Charlie
0 7496 2588 0 (hbk) 0 7496 3126 0 (pbk)

19th-CENTURY HISTORY

The Runaway Slave
A Tale of the British Slave Trade
0 7496 3093 0 (hbk)

The Sewer Sleuth
A Tale of Victorian Cholera
0 7496 2590 2 (hbk) 0 7496 3128 7 (pbk)

Convict!
A Tale of Criminals Sent to Australia
0 7496 2591 0 (hbk) 0 7496 3129 5 (pbk)

The Great Raj
A Tale about the British in India
0 7496 3090 6 (hbk)

Farewell to Ireland
A Tale of Emigration to America
0 7496 3094 9 (hbk)

The Great Hunger
A Tale about Famine in Ireland
0 7496 3095 7 (hbk)

Fire Down the Pit
A Tale of a Welsh Mining Disaster
0 7496 3091 4 (hbk)

TRAVELS OF A YOUNG VICTORIAN

1. The Golden Key
0 7496 2360 8 (hbk) 0 7496 2632 1 (pbk)

2. Poppy's Big Push
0 7496 2361 6 (hbk) 0 7496 2633 X (pbk)

3. Poppy's Secret
0 7496 2374 8 (hbk) 0 7496 2634 8 (pbk)

4. The Lost Treasure
0 7496 2375 6 (hbk) 0 7496 2635 6 (pbk)

20th-CENTURY HISTORY

Fight for the Vote
A Tale about the Suffragettes
0 7496 3092 2 (hbk)

The Road to London
A Tale of the Jarrow March
0 7496 2609 7 (hbk) 0 7496 3132 5 (pbk)

The Sandbag Secret
A Tale about the Blitz
0 7496 2608 9 (hbk) 0 7496 3133 3 (pbk)